THIS BOOK BELONGS TO

..............................................................................

Written by Tim Bugbird.
Illustrated by Nadine Wickenden.
Designed by Annie Simpson.

# The love in my heart

Tim Bugbird • Nadine Wickenden

make
believe
ideas

Big and Boo were resting,
after bouncing in the forest all day.
They were a long way from home
and Boo was very tired.

"I don't think I can make it all the way back to the burrow," said Boo. "My paws are just too sore!"

Big smiled and took Boo's hand.
"Well, I know you can,
and do you know why?"
said Big.

"Because with love in our hearts, we can do anything!"

As they walked, Big began to explain . . .

The love in our hearts could scent every flower.

The love
in our hearts
could cloak every tree.

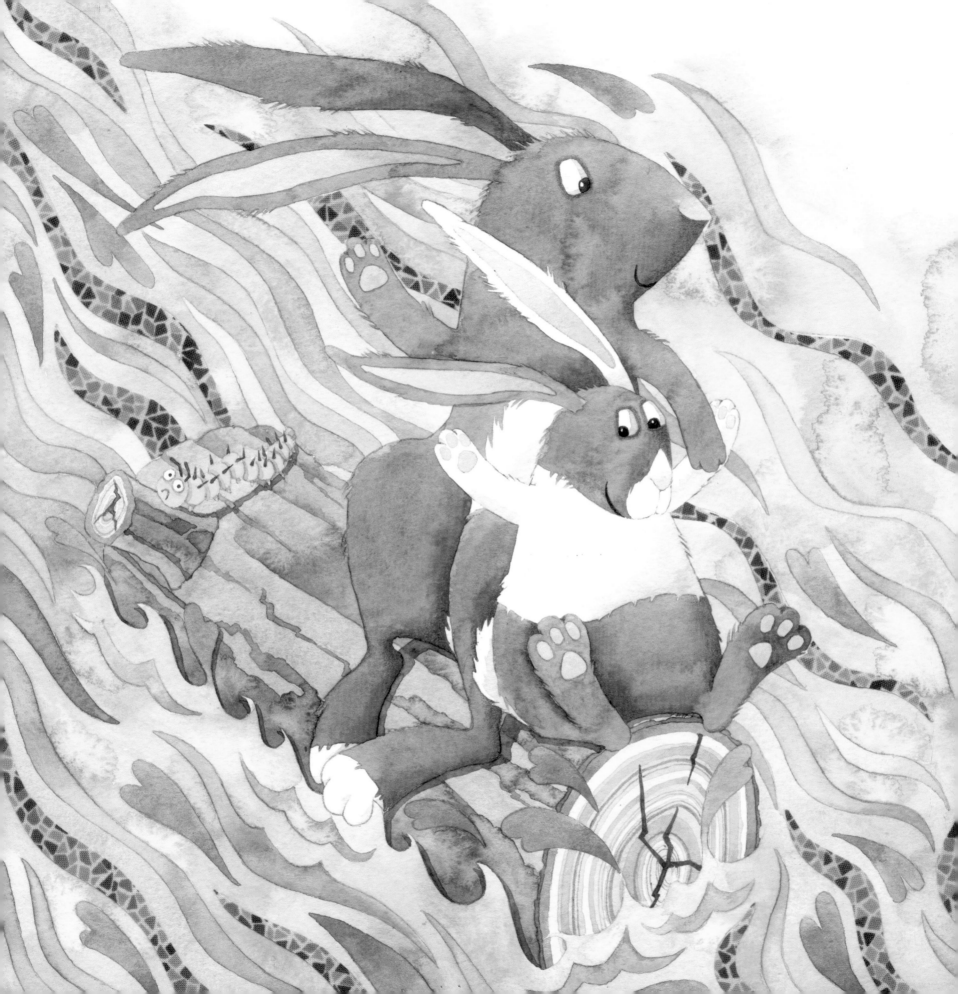

There's no doubt in my mind,

we could fill every river

with ripples of love,

all the way to the sea.

The love
that we share
could color
a rainbow,

with **plenty**

left over to

**light** up the sky.

And the **love** in our hearts

could cap every mountain

with soft, snowy blankets

of caring piled high.

The love
in our hearts
could change thunder
to song,

and **carpet** a pathway,

**no matter** how long.

The love in our hearts
could turn gray skies to blue.

With love we can do anything,
just me and you!

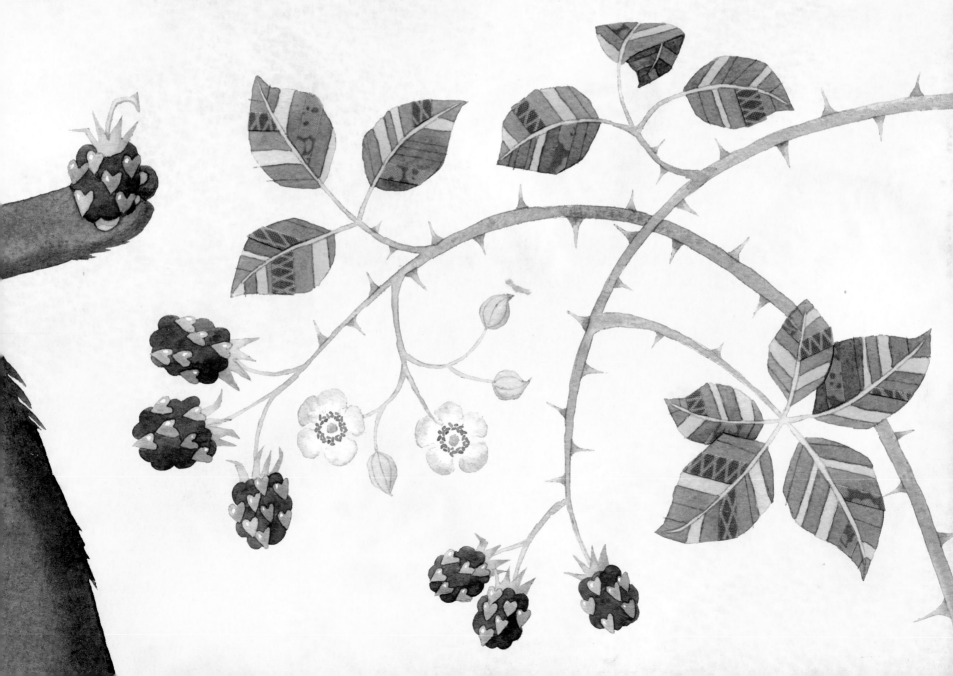

And before they knew it,
Big and Boo were home,
snuggled up in their cozy burrow.
"I love you,"
whispered Big.
But Boo was sound asleep.

THE END